For Imani Whyte—
one of New York City's beautiful little black diamonds in the rough
—*NG*

For my first A B C—
my father, Arthur B. Cummings
—*PC*

Text copyright © 1995 by Nikki Grimes, illustrations copyright © 1995 by Pat Cummings
All rights reserved
For information about permission to reproduce selections from this book,
please contact permissions@highlights.com.

Wordsong • An Imprint of Highlights
815 Church Street • Honesdale, Pennsylvania 18431
Printed in the United States of America

Library of Congress Cataloging-in-Publication Data
Grimes, Nikki.
C is for city / by Nikki Grimes ; illustrated by Pat Cummings.— 1st pbk. ed. [40] p. : col. ill. ;   cm.
Originally published: NY: Lothrop, Lee & Shepard, 1995.
Summary: Rhyming verses describe different aspects of life in a city, featuring each letter of the alphabet.
ISBN: 978-1-59078-013-8
1. City and town life — Juvenile literature.  2. English language — Alphabet — Juvenile literature.
[1.  City and town life.  2.  Alphabet.] I. Cummings, Pat, ill.  II. Title.  811.54   21   2002   CIP
2001086522
First Boyds Mills Press paperback edition, 2002

20 19 18 17 16 15 14 13 12 11

# C is for CITY

## NIKKI GRIMES & PAT CUMMINGS

### WORDSONG

Honesdale, Pennsylvania

A is for arcade or ads for apartments
on short streets with alleys alive with stray pets.
A is for Afghans named after their owners
who drive them to art shows in silver Corvettes.

B is for butcher or
breakfast with bagels
or block-party bands
out on hot summer nights.

C is for city or
cabbies named Clarence
or cool cats who chat
under boulevard lights.

D is for deli or doughnuts worth dunking
or doormen who jump double-Dutch while outside.
D is for drummers in dark-shaded glasses
who dazzle street-corner crowds from far and wide.

E is for El train,
for elders, and Easter,
for chrome elevators
with silvery walls.

F is for fire escape,
fruit stand, or factory,
for frail fortune-tellers
with fake crystal balls.

G is for gumball machines
at the grocer's
or for ghetto-blaster sounds
splitting the air.

H is for handball,
for hopscotch, and hot dogs,
for Hasidim in black hats
with dark curly hair.

I is for Italian ices in autumn
or ice-skating rinks when the weather turns cold.
I is for icicles on trees at Christmas
right next to department stores where toys are sold.

J is for jump shot,
for jacks on the sidewalk,
for jungle-gym climbing,
for jukebox, and jewel.

K is for kosher shops
selling knishes,
for kickball, and kite-flying
runs after school.

L is for latchkey or loud-laughing ladies
who lean out their windows and shout down the block.
L is for laundry day down at the Laundromat
where you can wash and dry clothes round the clock.

M is for majorette,
music, and marching bands
matching their steps
to the drum major's beat.

N is for newsstand
and neon lights blinking,
for nightclubs where folks
from the neighborhood meet.

O is for opera, for old-fashioned orange juice
whipped till it's foamy and spills out the glass.
O is for oboes at great outdoor concerts
with Mozart and picnic food right on the grass.

P is for playground or Pop's Pizzeria,
for piping hot pretzels with salt by the pound.
P is for pitching a bright copper penny
as far as you can before it hits the ground.

Q is for quarters
in gray parking meters,
for strolling quartets
harmonizing on key.

R is for ribs broiled
at cookouts in August
on roofs made of tar
that's as hot as can be.

S is for stickball or strawberry snow cones
or skyscrapers soaring straight up to the sun.
S is for sitting on stoops while the street sweeper
borrows your skateboard and rides it for fun.

T is for turnstile and trains full of tourists,
for tough-talking boys with steel taps on their shoes.
T is for taxi and two-story town houses
next door to temples with hard, wooden pews.

U is for unending trips Grandma takes you on
to new-and-used shops with cats on the stair.
U is for unwrapping umpteen small treasures
that uncanny Grandmother always finds there.

V is for vine-covered
Victorian houses
where vermilion leaves
slowly creep up the wall.

W is for watching
those brave window washers
who dangle from buildings
a million feet tall.

X is for X-ray shots
taken in hospitals
or for old xylophones
found in toy chests.

Y is for yams on the
Thanksgiving table,
for yellow school buses,
and yo-yo contests.

Z is for zillions of churches named Zion
in used-to-be storefronts just bursting with song.
Z is for zoo and the zebras you see there
when school term is over and you say "SO LONG!"

BRONX ZOO

MOUNTAIN ZEBRA
PLAINS ZEBRA
GREVY'S ZEBRA

# How many of these did you find?

**A**bstract painting, acrobat, acorn, address, Afghan hound, African mask, airplane, angel, angelfish, angora sweater, apartment ad, apple, arc, arcade, arch, Louis Armstrong, arrow, art, astronaut, auto, awning

**B**agel, balloon, banana, band, bangle, bead, bee, bell, block party, bow, bracelet, breakfast, bubble gum, bugle, butcher, button

**C**abby named Clarence, cactus, cap, card, cat, checkers, city, cloud, cool cat, constellation

**D**aisy, dark-shaded glasses, deli, dessert, diamond, dice, dime, dish, dish towel, dollar, doorman, dot, double-Dutch jump, doughnut, dragonfly, dreadlocks, drip, drummer, duck, dunking

**E**arth, Easter basket, Easter bonnet, Easter bunny, Easter egg, earring, eight, el train, elbow, elder, electrical cord, electrical outlet, elevator, Elvis Presley, embroidery, Empire State Building, *Entertainment*, eye, eyebrow

**F**abric, factory, fake crystal ball, fan, feather, finger, fingernail, fire escape, fish, flag, floor, flower, fortune teller, freckle, fringe, fruit stand, fur

**G**arden, gate, ghetto blaster, gift, giraffe pattern, glasses, goldfish, graffiti, *Glenn*, grape, grapefruit, grasshopper, greens, grocer, gumball

**H**air, halter top, hammer, hand, handball, hard hat, Hasidim, hat, headphones, heart, hexagon, hill, hopscotch, hula hoop, hydrant

**I**, ice, ice-cream cone, ice skater, icicle, igloo, inch, insect, instrument, island, Italian ice, italics, *Italy*, ivy

**J**acks, jellybean, jewel, jogger, juggler, jukebox, jump rope, jump shot, jungle gym

**K**angaroo, kettle, key, keyhole, kickball, kilt, kitchen, kite, knapsack, knish, knife, kosher

**L**ace, laces, ladder, ladybug, lamp, latchkey, laundry, Laundromat, lean, leaf, leggings, lemon, leopard spots, leotard, letter, lily pad, lion, locket, lollipop, loud-laughing ladies

**M**acy's department store, magazine, magnifying glass, majorette, man, map, marbles, marching band, mother, moon, mouse, mustache, music, mystery

**N**apkin, *Nature*, nautilus shell, neck, neckerchief, necklace, necktie, nectarine, needle, Nefertiti, neighborhood folks, neon light, *Neptune*, nest, net, *Network*, newspaper, newsstand, nickel, night, nightclub, *Nightlife*, *Nile*, nine, noodles, *North*, nose, notes, notebook, *Now*, numbers, nurse, nutcracker, nut, *NYC*

**O**boe, octagon, old-fashioned orange juice, opera, orange, orchestra, orchid, ostrich feather, opal, onyx, outdoor concert

**P**ail, paisley, palm tree, pants, parent, *Paris*, patch, pearl, penny, pickle, pigtails, pinwheel, piping-hot pretzel, pizza, plaid, plant, playground, Plaza Hotel, ponytail, polka dot, poodle, pool, popcorn, Pop's Pizzeria, postcard, pregnant, puddle, puffin, puzzle pieces

**Q**uack, quarter, quartet, queen, question mark, quiche, *quiet*, quilt, quotation mark

**R**abbit, rainbow, rattle, red, ribbon, ribs, rice, ring, rock, roof, rose

**S**andal, seashell, seven, shirt, shadow, shoe, shorts, sidewalk, skateboard, skyscraper, sleeve, snake, sneaker, sock, spot, stained glass, star, stoop, stick, stone, stop sign, straw, strawberry snowcone, street sweeper, string, stripes, sun, sunglasses

**T**ap, tape, taxi, teddy bear, teeth, telephone, temple, ten, tennis racquet, thorn, tie, tie-dyed shirt, tiger stripes, tiles, *Times Square*, token, top hat, tote bag, tough-talking boy, tourist, train, *trash*, trash can, tree, triangle, trombone, trousers, T-shirt, tulip, turnstile, turtleneck, tutu, tuxedo, tweed, twins, two, two-story townhouse

**U**dder, UFO, *Ugly Duckling*, ukelele, Ukrainian Easter egg, *Ulysses*, umbrella, uncanny grandmother, Uncle Sam, unicorn, unicycle, urn

**V** formation, valentine, van, vermilion leaves, Verrazano Narrows Bridge, vine-covered Victorian house

**W**allet, water, watermelon, wave, weather vane, whale, wheel, whiskers, whistle, wind chimes, Windsurfer, windmill, window, window washer, wood, *Wonder Windows*, wristwatch

**X**, X-ray, xylophone

**Y**am, yarn, yawn, yell, yellow school bus, yo-yo

**Z**ebra, zero, zigzag, Zion church, zipper, Zone, Zoo, Zoom

The illustrations of the letters of the alphabet are based on the following typefaces:

Airkraft, Benguiat, Cooper Black, Desdemonia Solid, Egyptian Outline, Frankfurter Medium, Goudy Heavyface Condensed, Highlander Bold Italic, Italia, Jellybean, Kable, Legacy, Masquerade, Neon, Ozwald, Palatino, Quorum, Rockwell, Souvenir Bold, Tiffany Heavy, Umbra, Venus, Windsor Bold, Xavier, Yankee Shadow, Zipper

Special thanks to Macy's, Northeast, Inc. for the use of the Macy's logo and building on page 20.